2 5 MAY 2021

1 5 JUL 2021

KT-434-914

To renew, find us online at: 12/20

https://capitadiscovery.co.uk/bromley

Please note: Items from the adult library
may also accrue overdue charges when
borrowed on children's tickets.

STRIPES PUBLISHING LTD
An imprint of the Little Tiger Group
1 Coda Studios
189 Munster Road,
London SW6 6AW

A paperback original
First published in Great Britain in 2020

ISBN: 978-1-78895-204-0

A CIP catalogue record for this book
is available from the British Library.

Printed and bound in China.

The Forest Stewardship Council® (FSC®) is a global, not-for-profit organization
dedicated to the promotion of responsible forest management worldwide. FSC defines
standards based on agreed principles for responsible forest stewardship that are supported
by environmental, social, and economic stakeholders. To learn more, visit www.fsc.org

STP/ 1800/0303/1219

2 4 6 8 10 9 7 5 3 1

44 Tiny Secrets

Sylvia Bishop

Illustrated by Ashley King

LiTTLE TiGER

LONDON

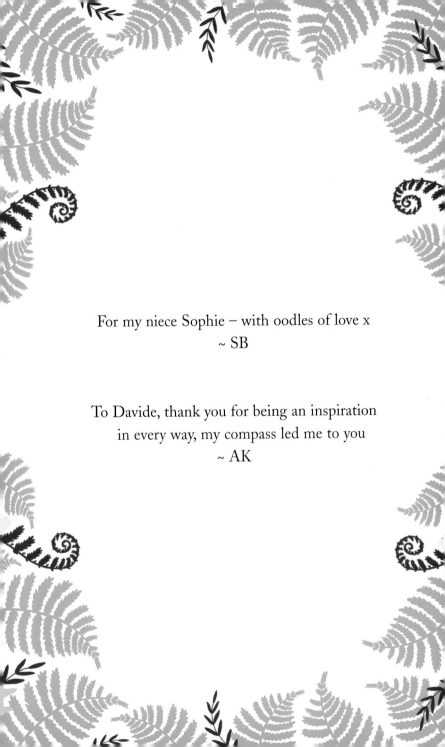

For my niece Sophie – with oodles of love x
~ SB

To Davide, thank you for being an inspiration
in every way, my compass led me to you
~ AK

CHAPTER ONE

A Terrible Disappointment

Betsy Bow-Linnet really wanted to kick something, just to make herself feel better. It had been a frustrating morning. But there was nothing in the room that she could sensibly kick:

Grand piano – too valuable

Rare and exotic ferns – too flimsy

Marble floor – too hard

Grandad – too alive

So instead, she took a very deep breath, which smelled of ferns. Then she put her fingers back on the piano keys and tried again. And yet again, it came out all wrong, with a rude kersplunk where the tune should have been. This time she did kick the piano – just a little bit. She wasn't wearing any shoes, so on balance this hurt her more than the piano.

"Ow," she announced.

"Everything all right, B?" came her grandad's voice from behind a fern frond. (There were an unbelievable number of ferns in the Bow-Linnets' parlour. Her mother liked ferns, too much. You couldn't sit anywhere without fronds waving in your face.)

"Yes thanks, Grandad."

"It's sounding very nice."

Betsy knew that was a lie. Her playing never sounded nice. Her mother, Bella Bow-Linnet, was a very brilliant concert pianist. Her father, Bertram Bow-Linnet, was also a very brilliant concert pianist. Grandad was brilliant too, although not quite as brilliant as his daughter and son-in-law. It was only Betsy who was no good. But she needed to become good – very good – before her parents got back from New York. That gave her precisely one week.

There was the rustle of a newspaper being put down, then Grandad got up from his armchair and his eyes appeared over the top of a fern. "Quick break for some biscuits, B?" he said.

"I'm all right, thanks."

"Just a very quick biscuit," he said firmly. "And a cup of tea." He was zigzagging through the plants and heading for the door before Betsy could protest. "I'll be back in a jiffy."

Betsy turned back to the piano and tried one more time.

Tinkle-TINK, tinkle-TINK, tinkerSPLUNKETT-SPLUNKle-splunkle— OW!

The 'ow' was Betsy after she kicked the piano again. Harder this time. She rubbed her foot tenderly. It hurt quite badly, and since she had been practising all morning with no success, she gave in for the time being.

She hobbled over to one of the elegant armchairs in among the ferns and waited for the sounds of slippered footsteps and rattling crockery. Grandad could even make carrying a tea tray sound like music. He took forever, but when he came back he had Jaffa cakes, which were Betsy's favourite. There was a pot of tea for him, and some lemonade for her.

"Now, Miss Betsy Bow-Linnet," said Grandad. "Are you going to tell me what on earth you're doing?"

Betsy nibbled a Jaffa cake in what she hoped was a carefree sort of way, and said, "Practising."

"I noticed," said her grandad. He always flapped his elbows up and down as he talked – Betsy used to think that was how he breathed. He flapped them accusingly at her now. "To be more precise, you've

been practising since seven in the morning on the first day of your summer holidays, when you would normally be in bed with a book until noon. So I suspect –" he poured himself some tea – "that you have some beans to spill…"

Betsy looked at her feet, partly to avoid looking at Grandad, and partly to see if she had a bruise coming on her big toe. It really hurt.

"So," said Grandad. "Spill them. It's just you, me and a small army of ferns."

Betsy didn't know what to say. She loved her grandad. Her parents were away so often that a few years ago he had moved in with them to help look after her. Betsy had always told him anything and everything. But just thinking about last night made her chest hurt, and she didn't want to say it out loud. At last she said,

"I just want to be a better pianist."

Grandad raised his eyebrows and elbows in unison. "Why?"

She shrugged.

"I've told you before, B," he said, more gently. "You don't have to like the piano. No one will mind if you don't."

That made Betsy's chest hurt even more than her foot, because Grandad's voice was so kind, but she knew that it wasn't true. Her mother minded and her father minded. And she hadn't even realized until last night. She had gone to their bedroom to say goodnight and goodbye. They were packing their suitcases for the New York International Classical Three-Fingered Piano Contest. As she was about to knock, she had heard her name, and paused.

"I do still wonder if we should have taken Betsy this time," her mother had said.

"She'd hate it –" that was her father talking – "nothing but piano concerts from dawn to dusk."

"Oh, Bertie," her mother had said, and Betsy had heard a trembling sigh. "Do you think she's maybe just a late bloomer?"

"Bella, darling. No. Betsy just isn't a pianist." Then her mother had snuffled and said the words that hadn't left Betsy's head all night: "Oh dear, I suppose you're right. It's just such a Terrible Disappointment."

A Terrible Disappointment.

She, Betsy Bow-Linnet, was

a Terrible Disappointment.

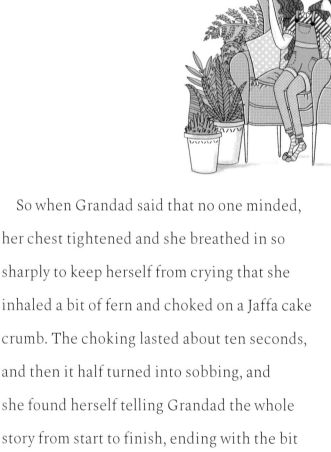

So when Grandad said that no one minded,
her chest tightened and she breathed in so
sharply to keep herself from crying that she
inhaled a bit of fern and choked on a Jaffa cake
crumb. The choking lasted about ten seconds,
and then it half turned into sobbing, and
she found herself telling Grandad the whole
story from start to finish, ending with the bit
where she would almost certainly never walk

again because she had broken her foot kicking the piano. Grandad didn't seem too worried about her foot, but his whole face melted and drooped when she told him about the Terrible Disappointment.

"Oh, B. I'm sure your mother didn't mean it," he said.

"She did. She sounded like she was almost crying. But it's all right," said Betsy. She scrubbed at her face fiercely and took another Jaffa cake for courage. Betsy Bow-Linnet might be a Terrible Disappointment but she was no coward. "By the time they get back, I'm going to be good at it. Really good."

Grandad looked worried.

"I am," said Betsy, determined.

"You know, Betsy," said Grandad, "your parents love you very much. I know they love their pianos too. But you matter much more – *people* that you love always come first."

"What about Grandma?" Betsy asked. As soon as the words left her mouth, she regretted them. "Sorry, Grandad," she said quickly. "I'm really sorry."

Before Grandma met Grandad, she had worked, lived and travelled with the circus. She loved her old life, but she gave it up for him, and for Betsy's mother. For a while. When Bella was seven, Grandma had left. Grandad always said that she couldn't help it: she loved them, but she loved the circus more.

Betsy wished she hadn't mentioned Grandma. She had said it without thinking. She was terrified that her parents loved pianos the way Grandma loved the circus – exclusively, untouchably, above all else. But it was selfish to bring it up.

She glanced over at her grandad, whose elbows were very still now as he sat and thought. Whenever Grandma was mentioned, Grandad seemed to shrink a little.

"It's all right, B," he said finally. "It's a good point. But your grandma was an unusual case." He was thinking. Betsy could always tell, because his elbows would go perfectly still and he would stick his head forward like a turtle. She waited. After a few seconds he drew his head back again: mind made up. "OK, Betsy. I'm going to help you. This week, we'll have a piano masterclass. But on one condition. If you're not quite as good as you'd like to be by the end of the week, you mustn't be worried or upset. Your parents will always be proud of you, whatever you do. Is that clear?"

Betsy nodded. She wasn't sure if she believed Grandad about the last bit, but she did want his help.

"I have two rules," he said. He held up one finger. "Rule number one: never practise anything at full speed until you can get all the notes right at half speed. Promise?" Betsy promised. "Good. Rule number two." He held up two fingers and looked sternly at his granddaughter. "Don't kick the piano."

And they both laughed, which made her feel a bit better. Then he gave her a hug, which made her feel a lot better. But after that, the real work began.

Grandad didn't mess around when it came to music. For the first three days, Betsy wasn't even allowed to play the piece she had been trying to learn. She was only allowed exercises.

Exercises for the left hand, exercises for the right.

Exercises at the top of the piano, and exercises down at the bottom.

Exercises to make her fingers nimble, and to teach her to go *ladiDA* with one hand and *TUMittytum* with the other at the same time.

Betsy hated exercises. It was hard to keep Grandad's second rule sometimes.

Then, with four days to go, she started learning the music. Grandad played it first, so that she could hear how it was all meant to fit together. He played beautifully, elbows floating with the rises and falls, and normally

Betsy loved to listen. But now, all she could think about was how different it was from her kersplunking version.

Lummittytummittytum, went Grandad.

Lummitysplunklebother, went Betsy.

She was learning Chopin's Mazurka in B flat. This is a very difficult and impressive sort of piece, but when you are a Bow-Linnet, you have to do something very impressive indeed to live up to expectations. Betsy learned it one tiny section at a time, at half speed as she had promised. Her fingers fumbled over the keys hopelessly, like worms on roller skates, but Grandad was endlessly patient.

"From the top, B," he would say. "It's sounding lovely."

With three days to go until her parents

returned, Betsy could get it right from beginning to end about half of the time. The other half of the time she would still kersplunk somewhere in the middle. Whenever she did, she felt her chest tighten and all she could think about was what a Terrible Disappointment she would be.

"From the top, B. It's sounding lovely," Grandad would say again.

And then the next time she would get it right. And so on.

Her parents called every day, asking how she was and what news she had. Betsy kept her replies vague. She wanted it to be a surprise.

When they called that evening, they told her there was going to be a party the evening they got back. They loved throwing parties. They were enormously popular. Crowds of elegant people would waft through the ferns drinking champagne, while some of the finest pianists in London took turns at the piano.

With one day to go, Betsy could get it right three times out of four. "I'm going to play it for them at the party," she told Grandad.

"Good idea, B," he said. But he looked worried.

"Do you think I shouldn't?"

"Of course you should. It's sounding lovely. From the top now." Betsy didn't know if she believed him, but there was nothing else to do but start again.

That evening, Grandad wanted Betsy to take a break, but Betsy was too fidgety to do anything but play the piano. So Grandad sighed and went flapping upstairs to his study, then huffing back down again with a stack of music. "No more Mazurka," he said. "You'll drive yourself crazy. Let's play duets."

Betsy loved playing with Grandad. Her notes got swept up in his, and it was like

they were dancing together. And sometimes
he would make up stupid song lyrics to sing
as they played, and he would keep going
until she was laughing too much to get the
notes right.

Tonight she laughed and laughed and
laughed, and it did help her feel less nervous
– until they stopped and she went to bed,
and there was nothing to listen to or laugh
at. In the silence, she played the Mazurka
with her fingertips against the mattress.

The next day, when her parents were
due home, Betsy couldn't get it right at all.
Grandad said it was just nerves, and that
she'd be all right on the night. He told her to
stop practising and help him water the ferns.
They'd both forgotten about them all week
and they were looking a bit droopy.

Betsy was just
watering the last
one – a small
maidenhair fern
outside Grandad's
study – when she
heard the front

door opening. Elegant
heels tapped on to the hallway's marble
floor, followed by the *clippity-clip* of shiny
leather brogues. Together, they tapped out
a perfectly timed duet, brought to a close by
the thud of large bags on the marble floor.
Betsy's heart thumped.

"Betsy, darling?" called her mother.

"B?" called her father.

The tapping feet came to a halt.

"We're home!"

CHAPTER TWO

A Terrible Mess

From above, Mr and Mrs Bow-Linnet looked like this:

When most people think of their parents, they picture their faces. Betsy always thought of the tops of her parents' heads. This was the view she had when she stuck her legs through the spindles of the balcony on the top floor of their house and watched them leave for a concert, or welcome guests to a party, or come home late at night when she was meant to be asleep.

That's what she could see now, as they whirled about getting ready for the party. She had hidden herself up in her favourite spot by the balcony rails to avoid answering questions about how she had spent her week, and whether she had been good, and whether she was feeling all right. When her parents had first arrived she had gone downstairs to see them from the front, of course.

This is what they looked like from Betsy's height:

Bella Bow-Linnet looked remarkably like a
fern. Her fronds of hair curled and her tiny smile
curled and she curled her body around when
she talked, swaying with enthusiasm. She even
smelled like ferns – but then, that will happen,

if you live with so many for so long.

Bertram Bow-Linnet was as stiff and straight as his wife was curly. He always had a neat pocket handkerchief and neatly shined shoes, and he lived a life of mystery behind his beard. Betsy could never be quite sure what he was feeling.

It was wonderful to have them home, and for an hour she had had them all to herself, and they had all eaten cream cakes (which were Bertram's favourite) while her parents told stories about New York. But now there was a party to prepare, so Betsy watched and waited above.

The parties always took a lot of preparation. It used to just be her parents' pianist friends who came to play for each other, but over time word spread and now all the stylish-and-wealthy of London came to hear these great musicians. This meant that the house always had to be spruced up so that none of the stylish-and-wealthy would have to confront anything unseemly, like used teacups, or old newspapers, or dust. The Bow-Linnets' house was Bertram's childhood home, and it was a very grand London townhouse, but it wasn't always very tidy.

As Betsy watched from her perch, the grey egg of her father's head left the hall, and a moment later the pink egg of Grandad entered. This is what Grandad looked like from above:

Betsy hardly ever saw Grandad from above. It made him look fragile. He carefully carried piles of plates and glasses to the parlour for the party, whistling to himself.

There was a *thu-thu-thud*, like a gigantic pack of cards being shuffled. That was the sound of the folding door being pushed back between the parlour and the lower sitting room to create one enormous room, which was perfect for parties. When the furniture from the lower sitting room was moved to the side, you could fit a lot of people in there. Betsy gripped the balcony, her palms sweating at the thought of all those people listening to her play. She shut her eyes and tapped the Mazurka out against the wood.

Finally, every last corner had been dusted and every last fern had been extra-watered, and the house was ready. Betsy was sent to put on her best dress.

Her mother came to do her hair. Betsy had inherited Bella's curls, but on her they were less like fern fronds and more like a gorse bush in outer space. Bella was the only person who could tame them. As Betsy sat in front of the mirror, it occurred to her that her mother must know the top of her head best too. She had never seen the top of her own head. She hoped it wasn't too untidy.

"Is everything all right, darling? You've been very quiet."

"Yes thanks."

"Did you have a nice time while we were away?"

Betsy thought no and said yes, which was uncomfortable. She never normally lied about how she felt, and her mother was brilliant at making her feel better, curling around her in an enormous hug and talking everything over until Betsy felt still and calm again. But this time Bella was the problem – or rather, Betsy was – so she had to lie.

"Good. Betsy darling, you really must brush your hair every day. This is a terrible mess."

Terrible Mess, Terrible Disappointment. Betsy, seen from above.

With quarter of an hour to go, Betsy's
father came to give her a flower for her
hair. He did that every time she was getting
dressed up for something. Her smart dress
was nice – dark blue and swirly – but she
liked the flower best.

"Is this the room of Miss Betsy Bow-
Linnet?" he said gravely.

Betsy grinned and nodded.

"Would she do me the honour of wearing
this flower in her hair tonight?" He bent
down so that his eyes were level with hers
behind his half-moon spectacles. "Beautiful,
B," he said, tucking the lily in place. Betsy
thought that if he asked if she was all
right, she might just tell him the truth.
After all, he hadn't said she was a Terrible
Disappointment. But he didn't ask.

With five minutes to go, they were all lined up in the hall, waiting for the doorbell to ring.

"Everything all right, B?" said Grandad.

"Yes," said Betsy, a little too loudly.

Grandad leaned closer and whispered, "Remember that second rule. It's very bad form to kick a piano during a concert."

He smiled, but Betsy only had time for half a smile before the doorbell rang. Once it had rung the first time, it kept ringing. An endless river of people trickled along the hallway and flooded the parlour. Bella would hug them and Bertram would shake them neatly by the hand. Then it would be Betsy's turn, and they would all exclaim about how much she had grown, and talk to her in silly syrup voices with silly huge smiles.

Grandad didn't have to hug them or shake
their hands or be introduced. He hated
these parties and, as usual, he was doing
an excellent job of pretending to be a fern

and avoiding the whole situation. A woman in purple silk came in, and while Bella and Bertram greeted her, Grandad made a face at Betsy and looked like a fern harder than ever.

"And you remember Betsy, Vera," said her mother to the column of purple.

Vera Brick was one of Betsy's all-time least favourite people. She beamed down at the air just above Betsy's head. "Oh my," she declared. "I wouldn't have recognized her, Bella." (She never talked directly to Betsy.) "Hasn't she grown? Why, she'll be taller than all the boys, if she isn't careful." She laughed. When Vera laughed, it was one single joyless chirp. It sounded so much like the doorbell that Bertram opened the door. He blinked at the empty doorstep, pushed up his spectacles, and shut the door again with a sheepish *ahem*.

"Still," said Vera, "long limbs come with long fingers I suppose. When will she be dazzling us in the concert halls of London, hmm?" And she chirped again. Bella laughed politely and steered Vera towards the canapés in the parlour. "Oh my, the poor ferns," Betsy heard Vera wail. "They're positively drooping. They can't have been watered for weeks."

Betsy and Grandad exchanged glances. Betsy decided that if she really needed to kick something that evening, she would just kick Vera.

It didn't take long for the piano-playing to start. All of London's best pianists were here, and quite a lot of other people who fancied their chances. Betsy noticed nervously that although everyone smiled and clapped ever so politely, they were all whispering reviews to each other afterwards.

"A rather clunking left hand."

"My, how original to play the whole thing at one volume."

"Well at that speed, a three-year-old could play it."

And so on.

Betsy waited patiently. There seemed to be two ways to get your turn on the piano:

1. Squeal "Me, me!" and run over madly. Be sure to wave your champagne glass to remind everyone that you are tipsy, and that you would never push yourself forward if you weren't.

2. Wait for someone else to bray your name. Refuse for approximately 2.3 seconds, look awfully embarrassed (as if you couldn't possibly), then graciously accept. End up playing five pieces until eventually one of the squealers shoves you off the stool.

Betsy lost track of how many hours she spent listening to waltzes and minuets, nocturnes and etudes, squealing and braying and wicked whispering. After what seemed like a few weeks of it, Grandad stopped pretending to be a fern and came to stand next to her.

"Do you still want to play, B?"

She didn't. But that was neither here nor there. Betsy Bow-Linnet might be a Disappointment, and a Mess, but she was not a coward. So she nodded.

"You could always play for them after the party."

"I want to play now."

"That's my girl." Grandad squeezed her shoulder. And when the next piece had marched triumphantly to a halt, he bellowed,

"Betsy! Let's hear Betsy."

A murmur of surprise rippled around the parlour. Everybody clapped, and joined in calling her name, because nobody had ever heard the youngest Bow-Linnet play the piano. Across the room, Betsy saw that her parents' smiles were frozen in horror. She tried to smile encouragingly at them, to let them know that it was going to be fine – that she was a late bloomer, after all. She wasn't sure the smile had worked though. They didn't look as encouraged as she'd hoped.

"From the top now, B," Grandad whispered in her ear.

Betsy tapped across the marble floor to the piano stool and sat down. For one awful second, she couldn't make any sense of the piano keys. Then her fingers decided to get on with things without her and she found that they had put themselves in the right place.

Well done, fingers, she thought. *Now what?*

This, said her fingers. And they began.

CHAPTER THREE

A Terrible Tragedy

Betsy was confused.

She thought she had been note-perfect. Well maybe there had been an odd wrong note here and there, but no kersplunks. When she took her hands off the piano keys, she had been overjoyed. People had clapped. Out of the corner of her eye, she saw Grandad's elbows pumping out applause like bellows.

But as she looked around she realized,

with a sinking horror, that all the smiles were either fake or smug, that all the applause was just a polite patter, and that the whispering was beginning, vigorous and vicious. She looked at her parents. They were applauding her, hard – too hard – as if they thought they could clap the pattering applause up into a storm by themselves. But their smiles were forced and they weren't meeting anybody's eyes. Betsy wasn't fooled.

"Oh my. What an embarrassment," whispered Vera, very loudly.

Betsy's face burned. It somehow made it worse that she didn't know what she had done wrong. She wanted to run out of the room and hide. But even if Betsy Bow-Linnet was a Disappointment and a Mess and an Embarrassment, she was quite determined not to be a coward. So she squiggled a tiny bow, sort-of smiled, and walked as calmly as she could back to Grandad.

A moment later someone was squealing, "Me! Me!", champagne glass aloft, and the whole thing was over. Just like that.

"Did I do something wrong, Grandad?" Betsy whispered.

Grandad shook his head vigorously. "You were note-perfect."

"Then why did Vera say I was an Embarrassment?"

Grandad wafted his elbows in an enormous shrug. "Vera Brick," he said, "is a mystery to me." And after a moment's thought, he added, "And long may she remain so."

Betsy couldn't get anything but compliments out of Grandad, and she wanted the truth. She would have to ask her parents. But every time she looked for them, she found them caught in a different web of friends, and she couldn't get them alone. She tried not to believe they were doing it on purpose.

In the end she gave in and did her best to look like a fern and wait for the whole thing to be over. She wasn't as good at it as Grandad was. She was too wriggly to be very good at blending in. People kept noticing her, and saying things like "Good effort, dear" and "That was very brave of you", which were not real compliments. It seemed to be hours and hours before everyone finally began to trickle into the hall one by one, repeat all the hugging and handshaking, take their coats, and take their leave.

When the last guest had finally gone (saying "You looked very pretty at the piano, poppet" on her way out), Betsy hugged her mother for a long time.

"What did I do wrong, Mum?"

"Oh, darling," said her mother, curling around her sadly. "Nothing.

Nothing at all. People just had silly expectations."

"What expectations?"

But Bella said that the ferns were giving her hay fever and went upstairs to bed.

Betsy looked at her father. "Dad? I want to know what I did. Why was everyone whispering about me?"

Bertram looked as though he was going to tell her it was nothing too, but she did her fiercest face. So he sighed, bent down, and put his hands on her shoulders. "All right, B. You deserve to know what they were saying, but you must remember, their silly opinions don't matter. Even a little bit. You know that, yes?"

Betsy nodded.

Bertram paused, searching for the right

words, before he said, "You were note-perfect. But there's more to playing than getting the notes right. There's the passion, the rises and falls, the sense of the music." (He said this last part a bit wearily, as though he sometimes wished there wasn't quite so much passion.)

"And I didn't have that?"

"No, B," he said. Not unkindly. "But it doesn't matter, you know, it really doesn't. You mustn't worry about it for a second –" and he gave her an earnest sort of hug.

"Vera Brick said I was an Embarrassment."

"She was wrong."

"Mum doesn't get hay fever."

Bertram opened his mouth, changed his mind, shut it again, and opened it in a new shape. "Your mother is very tired from the trip." There was a long silence. Sometimes Bertram had trouble thinking of the right thing to say. So Betsy gave up waiting for any further explanation, hugged him goodnight, and went upstairs to bed.

From his study across the landing, Grandad came out with cheerful elbows and more compliments. Betsy said a hasty goodnight and hid herself in her room.

She didn't sleep for a long time.

The next day, her parents pretended very hard that nothing bad had happened. Bella took her out for milkshakes, and on the way back they stopped at Betsy's favourite pet shop to look at all the animals, and Bella let her spend ages and ages saying hello to every last hamster and rabbit and stick insect. She was being so kind and trying so hard to take Betsy's mind off things, that it was difficult to believe that Betsy really did disappoint her. If only, Betsy thought, she hadn't overheard that one small sentence.

By the evening, she had half decided to just put up with being a Disappointment. She snuck out of bed when she was meant to be asleep and dangled her legs through the banisters, to take a reassuring look at her world below. The heads of her mum and dad and grandad still criss-crossed along the hall, and the ferns still swayed, and the black and white spirals on the marble floor still looked like they were swirling if you squinted at them a bit funny. Nothing had really changed. She could just forget. She watched the parlour light go out, and then the light in Grandad's study opposite, and finally she went back to bed.

Perhaps that would have been the end of it all, if it hadn't been for the next day's edition of the *London Natter*.

It was Vera Brick who brought a copy over. Bertram, Bella, Betsy and Grandad had just finished lunch and were rounding it off with tea and cake, when she stopped by – "Just for the smallest of seconds" – and unfurled the paper on the table with a flourish. She said she thought they ought to know.

"I *mean*," she exhaled, woe-struck. And she clasped her hands to her bosom, to show just how much she meant it. But what exactly she meant was still a mystery.

Bertram pulled the paper closer, looked

at it over his spectacles, and read the page's title out loud:

⇉LONDON NATTER⇇

FIFTY HATS YOU MIGHT NOT REALIZE ARE HATS (THAT YOU CAN BUY FOR LESS THAN A YACHT!)

"No, no," said Vera, sounding just a smidge less woe-struck and the tiniest bit impatient. "Not that. The gossip column."

The *London Natter*'s gossip column was the most colossal waste of paper ever invented. It commented on the rich and famous in London – what they had been wearing, who they had been dating, what colour they'd painted their front doors, how they took their tea. Bertram looked at it uncertainly, coughed, and obediently began to read about Celia Botherdown's weekend in Scarborough.

"This," announced Grandad, "is extremely tedious."

"Keep going, Bertie," urged Vera. So Bertram read about the birthday party of the youngest child of Clara and Clarence How-Lavverly. Little Miss How-Lavverly had worn a dress made of sequins sewn together by specially trained spiders using their own thread.

"Really, Vera," said Bella delicately. "Where is this—"

"SHH," said Vera. *Almost* rudely.

Bertram rolled on as if nobody had interrupted. "While one child sparkled this weekend, another certainly did not."

He hesitated then, and looked at Betsy.

"Read it, Dad," said Betsy quietly.

He dithered, then hesitated some more.

"I'd rather hear it from you," said Betsy, "than read it myself later."

"Well," said Bertram uncertainly. "It's a lot of rubbish, B." And then, very quickly and quietly, he read out: "Betsy Bow-Linnet, only daughter of noted concert pianists Bella and Bertram Bow-Linnet, stunned partygoers this Saturday with an entirely lifeless performance of Chopin's Mazurka in B flat. "It was completely robotistical," one guest confided to the *Natter*. "She hasn't got a drop of talent – such a tragedy." Our source adds that Betsy spent most of the night doing a very substandard impression of a fern."

There were hot tears in Betsy's eyes but she blinked them away. She was determined not to give Vera the satisfaction.

Bertram put the paper down and looked at them all. He frowned. He pushed his glasses up his nose. He cleared his throat. He said, "Is robotistical a word?"

Vera thought that was beside the point. For once, Betsy was inclined to agree with her.

"It is exactly the point," said Grandad, red in the face with annoyance. "The point being that this was written by an idiot, and it will be read by idiots, in one never-ending loop of astonishing idiocy."

"So true," agreed Vera, nodding vigorously, as if she herself never read the *Natter*. "I certainly wouldn't give it a moment's thought. I just thought Betsy should hear it from a friend," she added, looking compassionately at a patch of wall a little to the left of Betsy.

"Thank you, Vera, that's very thoughtful of you," said Bella. "Now, Betsy darling, you're not to worry about it." She put her lips into a smile. It looked like she was trying not to cry. "Let's all talk about something nicer."

Vera's mission of mercy was over but she carried on woozing around tragically until they offered her some tea and cake. That cheered her up sharpish. She still didn't show any sign of leaving, so Betsy asked to be excused and got up from the table. As she left, they all told her not to worry about the column. She nodded and promised that she wouldn't. But of course she did. It's difficult not to worry about being a Disappointment *and* a Mess *and* an Embarrassment *and* a Tragedy.

She worried about it all evening, and that night she stayed up so late worrying about it that she didn't wake up until very late the next day. Her parents had left her a note, explaining that they had gone to have coffee and cake with someone-or-other, and Grandad was outside gardening. (The garden and the shed were Grandad's territory, and he grew anything and everything out there apart from ferns.) When Betsy went downstairs, the huge house seemed very quiet and lonely. She felt like she didn't belong there any more. As if even the house knew that she wasn't a real pianist.

She pattered across the hall, heading towards the parlour – then stopped, surprised.

There was a letter for her on the doormat.

It had no stamp, and no address. Just her name, written in the blackest ink on a stiff cream envelope. "Huh," said Betsy. "That's strange."

This, she would soon learn, was a staggering understatement.

-BETSY-
BOW~LINNET

CHAPTER FOUR

GLORIA SPRIGHTLY

Betsy picked up the letter and was about to open it, but it felt wrong to tear it open in the hall. This was clearly a special sort of letter. So she ran up the stairs to the top floor and noodled her legs through the spindles of the banister. Here, in her favourite spot, she opened the envelope.

Dear Miss Bow-Linnet,

the letter began, in the blackest of ink on the very creamiest of stiff paper,

I had the pleasure of listening to you perform Chopin's Mazurka in B flat on Saturday night. I then had the immense displeasure of reading the London Natter yesterday. Frankly, I don't think robotistical is even a word.

Betsy's heart was pounding, but it paused its pounding for just a second to feel that this was *definitely* beside the point.

You played an extremely difficult piece. Any other child who could play so well at your age would be considered gifted, but because you are a Bow-Linnet, your hard work has been scorned. Miss Bow-Linnet, it is my opinion that this is deeply unfair, wildly unjust and unspeakably upsetting.

I would like to help. With my assistance, your next performance will be completely, totally, stupendously stunning. We would not need to meet. I can send my Method to you by post. However, I will need your word that you will not tell anyone, ever, about this Method. Not even your family. I will also need you to buy quite a lot of pumpkin seeds.

If you agree to these terms, please write to me at:

The Ivy Hotel, Mulberry Avenue, London, NW1 4ED

Please reply today - I will not be staying at The Ivy long. Ms Bow-Linnet, I eagerly, humbly and gut-flutteringly hope that you will accept my offer. I should warn you that my Method is somewhat unusual. Success, however, is absolutely guaranteed.

Yours with admiration and respect,

Gloria Sprightly

When Betsy had read it, she read it again to make sure. She tried reading it out loud, to see if that would help. It didn't. Her heart kept up the pounding, but in a rather confused sort of way, like a moth against a lamp. She didn't know what to make of it.

Gloria Sprightly. Betsy racked her brains to try and remember which of the faces at the party had been called Gloria. There had been so many of them and she had been so distracted. And why did Gloria, whoever she was, need pumpkin seeds to teach piano?

Betsy checked her watch. Her parents were due home in about fifteen minutes. If she was going to send a reply today without them asking any questions, she was going to have to act fast. There was no time for second thoughts. There wasn't really time for first thoughts. Thoughts were altogether off the agenda. So, as thoughtlessly as she could manage, Betsy found some notepaper and scribbled a reply:

Dear Ms Sprightly,

Thank you very much for your really kind letter. I would like to know what your Method is and I promise not to tell anyone. Pumpkin seeds should be fine.

Here she paused, trying to think of a good way to phrase the question that was jiggling around inside her head. It was hard to put into words. The closest she could get was 'But... WHAT?', or perhaps 'Are you mad?'. But neither of those questions belong in a letter to a stranger, and time was slipping away, so she had to make do with just signing her name.

Betsy Bow-Linnet

The only envelope she had was left over from her birthday party invitations – it had a picture of a lemur holding a balloon in the corner. It didn't look very Mysterious and Important, but she just had to hope that Gloria Sprightly wouldn't mind. She sealed the envelope and found a stamp.

With seven minutes to go, she put on her coat and sprinted to the postbox at the end of her road. She put the letter halfway in and froze, allowing a niggle of worry to bubble

63

up inside her. Then she reminded herself that Betsy Bow-Linnet was not a coward. She screwed up her courage, and her eyes, and her fists. She realized she was screwing up the letter too, so she unscrewed everything and posted the envelope through the slot.

She regretted it instantly but she didn't linger, for three very good reasons:

1. The letter was already in the belly of the postbox, and that was that.

2. Her parents would be home in four minutes.

3. It was starting to rain. Regret is miserable, but sodden regret is worse.

She turned and sprinted back home. Hurrying through the door, she shoved her wet coat to the back of the coat rack, grabbed a book at random off the parlour bookshelf, pushed through the ferns, threw herself into the nearest armchair, and looked at the page with rapt concentration. Just in time. A key turned in the lock.

"Hello, darling!"

"Hello, B!"

Betsy called *Hello* back, in an Oscar-worthy performance of a girl-who-has-been-in-her-chair-all-along. Her mother's footsteps retreated up the stairs but her father's came across the hall and into the parlour. They paused.

"B?" he said.

"Yes?"

Bertram squinted at her through the ferns. "Are you reading the London *A to Z*?"

Betsy realized that she was indeed looking at a map of London. Islington, to be precise. "Um," she said. "Yes."

"Righto," said her father. He sat down next to her with his paper, so Betsy had to carry on pretending to care deeply about the backstreets of Islington.

Even though she knew her letter could not

yet have reached Gloria, she found herself waiting all that afternoon and evening for something to happen – listening for a letter on the doormat, or a knock at the door, or … anything.

But of course, nothing did happen. Not until the next day.

She was awake bright and early, and crept down to snatch up any envelopes that arrived before her family could pick them up and start asking questions. But nothing had arrived, and nothing arrived all morning, and the afternoon rolled around and still nothing arrived. So when there was finally a gentle thud on the doormat, it took Betsy a moment to realize what it was.

She ran to the door. It was another stiff cream paper envelope, with the same black ink. No stamp: it had been posted by hand again.

Betsy ran up to her bedroom, tore open the envelope, and began to read.

Dear Betsy (may I call you Betsy?),

Hurray! Huzzah! Magnificent news! I will send you a parcel tomorrow morning. Please make sure you are in to receive it.

In the meantime, I'd like you to take a look at the piano in your parlour. Go to it now, please, and I'll explain some things to you.

Go on. This will be much more interesting if you go and have a look.

I hope you've gone.

Betsy hadn't, of course. But Gloria was insisting, so she pocketed the letter, ran all the way to the ground floor, and went into the

parlour. Nobody was there, so she took out
the letter again, and carried on reading.

*Thank you. Now, prop open the lid and take
a good look at the inside.*

A grand piano is shaped a bit like a
footprint. It has one very wide end, where the
keys are, and then a long narrower end. This
narrower end is covered by a lid, which can be
propped open with a special stick. Betsy did
this now, showing the belly underneath. This
is what she saw:

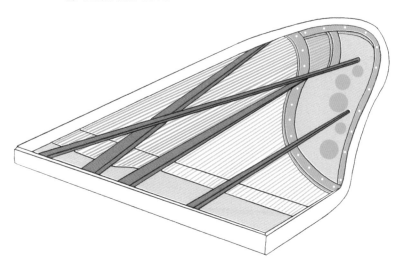

This is the soundboard, Betsy. Isn't it magnificent? Have a good look around. Every pianist should appreciate the beauty of their instrument.

You will see the strings stretched across it. Eighty-eight of them. You probably know that when you press a piano key, a hammer hits these strings, and that's what makes the sound. You can see the hammers at the back of the board play a note and watch what happens.

But how does the key move the hammer on to the string? This is where it all gets horrendously complicated, I'm afraid. Between the strings and the keys is the part called the action. It's impossibly tricky to see this, so I'll draw it for you:

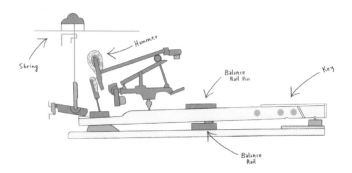

Alas, Betsy! Pianos are complicated. Here's another drawing of it with just the most important bits. This one's less likely to give you nightmares:

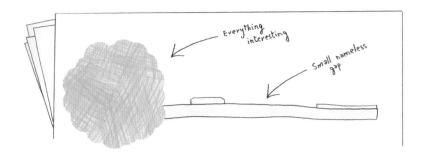

So you see, the piano keys are at one end of a seesaw. The middle of the seesaw is called the balance rail, topped by the balance rail pin. Everything Interesting, including the hammer, is on the other end. When the key-side goes down, Everything Interesting goes up, and the hammer hits the string.

Now, Betsy, if you look closely at the

diagram, you will see that there is a small gap between the key and the balance rail pin. You can't see it on your piano it's hidden under the panel. There's nothing there to see anyway. Here is a picture of it:

You see? Nothing there. But appearances aren't everything, Betsy. This is my favourite bit of the piano.

That's all. You can shut the lid now. Remember, you need to be in tomorrow morning to receive your parcel!

Yours with delight and excitement,

Gloria Sprightly

For a minute after reading the letter, Betsy carried on looking at the web of strings and wooden ridges and metal pins and strips of bright red felt. She had never really looked before. Gloria was right. It was magnificent.

Then she shut the lid and the soundboard vanished. In its place she could see her own face, looking back at her from the polished black surface. It was a puzzled face: a face that was wondering what all this had to do with anything, and what on earth the parcel might be.

She kept on wondering all day. She was so busy wondering that Grandad had to say "All right, B?" eight times before she heard him. She was so busy wondering she walked into three different ferns, which made them curl inwards sadly. She was awake half the night just wondering and dreaming up guesses.

None of her guesses were close.

CHAPTER FIVE

THE UNUSUAL METHOD

The following morning, Betsy was enjoying a
late breakfast when there was a knock on the
door. She opened it to find a parcel on the
doorstep.

Bella was out at a rehearsal, and Bertram was braving his monthly visit to his terrifying great-aunt Agatha. Betsy checked that Grandad was still in the garden: he was, happily pruning an obviously dead plant as though it might yet revive, and whistling to himself. The coast was clear.

She carried the box up to her bedroom. It was heavy, and her bedroom was on the second floor. She set it down with relief, shut the door, then carefully peeled back the paper.

Inside there was a glass tank, and inside the glass tank was a brown leather box with a carry handle, and on top of the brown leather box was a stiff cream envelope. She took out the envelope to read the letter first, because you should always begin with

the letter, but she was itching to open the
beautiful leather box.

Dear Betsy,

I hope you enjoyed looking at the piano.
Aren't they fascinating objects?

Please find enclosed forty-four African
pygmy mice.

(Betsy read that bit six times, but it carried
on saying the same thing.)

As you will see, they are in their travelling
case at the moment. They should live in the
tank most of the time. Please look after them
kindly I enclose instructions.

Do Not Handle the Mice.

They are so astonishingly small that you
can hurt them just by holding them. In fact,
you are the proud owner of forty-four of the
world's very smallest variety of mouse. They

are only one inch long. They are so small, they can fit in the hidden part between the key and the balance rail pin - my favourite part, if you remember. Here is a picture of one in the piano:

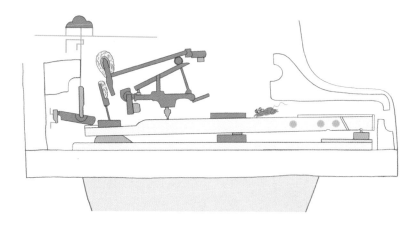

From here, they can press down the key-side of the seesaw, and that pushes Everything Interesting up. And when Everything Interesting goes up, as you know, the piano makes a sound.

Perhaps you have seen a well-trained dog, Betsy, or the clever tricks of circus animals? Here in this box you have forty-four stupendously well-trained mice. Each is in charge of two notes on the piano. I trained them using very small seesaws and a pumpkin seed reward system, but once they have heard the music, they will play it for its own sake. These mice **love** the piano. They are particularly fond of anything by Beethoven.

Still. A pumpkin seed after each performance wouldn't hurt.

Betsy, no human could ever play a piano quite like these mice. They are unbeatably nimble. They are exquisitely gentle. They have marvellously sensitive hearing. Try them out: you will see what I mean.

Instructions For a Pygmy Mouse Performance

Put the carry case on the soundboard, and say "play". This sends the mice running under the panel to their places. They can hide there for several hours quite happily, so simply find a private moment any time before the performance to release them.

I enclose a list of pieces they can play. Say the name of the piece exactly as written on the list, and they will begin.

Obviously, if anyone is watching, you will need to know the piece well enough to make the right sort of movements. The more closely you can mime it, the better - **but don't let anybody watch your hands.**

Say "home" to call them back. Make sure the box is ready, or they will run off trying to find it.

Enjoy the music. Bask in glory.

I realize that my Method may come as a bit of a surprise but I am certain that you will be delighted by the results. It is a trick, of course, but I am only too pleased to play a harmless trick on the sort of silly people who read the London Natter.

Good luck, Betsy!

Yours as ever, with anticipation and hope,

Gloria Sprightly

P.S. I must remind you, although my pen trembles at my boldness, that you have given your word to tell no one about this Method. This is **very** important. Betsy, I implore you to keep your word.

P.P.S. They are really (here Betsy had to turn the page over) very good at the Mazurka.

That was the end.

"Um," said Betsy, to the universe at large.

It seemed to her that the universe at large shrugged, as if it took no responsibility for Gloria Sprightly.

Betsy put down the letter and lifted the brown leather case out of the tank. The front had a glass window, and behind the glass were rows of tiny compartments. Underneath each compartment there were labels saying things like 'D flat and D second octave' and 'F and F sharp fourth octave' in tiny handwriting in the blackest ink.

As Betsy set the box down, forty-four astonishingly small noses came up to the glass, and quivered in a 'how-do-you-do' sort of way. Betsy lay down on her stomach to get a better look.

"Hello," she whispered.

Forty-four noses twitched, and eighty-eight pin-prick eyes blinked, in a silent hello-chorus.

"Do you play the piano?" said Betsy, in an even more wispy sort of whisper, because she felt a bit stupid for even asking. "Can you really? Or is Gloria completely mad?"

It almost looked as if forty-four heads nodded twice: yes, we can, and yes, she's mad. But it could have just been a united twitch. The trouble with being an inch long is that almost anything you do looks like it might have just been a twitch. The tiny mice looked up at her expectantly. Innocently.

"All right, mice," Betsy said sternly. "How do I know that you won't nibble the strings, or ... or..." She trailed off, because there are not many crimes that a mob of pygmy mice could commit. "Well anyway," she said, "I'm not going to risk putting you in the parlour piano. We should at least start you in the morning room piano. Just to be sure." The mouse-mob expressed no opinion on this either way, and there was no one else to ask. So after a few more minutes of staring and wondering, Betsy checked on Grandad out of the window, then picked up the travelling case and made her way carefully downstairs to the first floor.

The grand piano in the morning room was slightly less gobsmackingly valuable than all the other pianos that the Bow-Linnets owned. The frame had warped, just a fraction, and as a result it would never stay perfectly in tune for very long. It was kept under a dustsheet. The curtains were almost shut, letting in a single shaft of light which showed the dust in the air.

Betsy felt strangely sorry for that piano. She pulled off the cover, propped open the lid, and held up the cage of mice so that they could inspect it. "What do you reckon?" she said. "The F in the middle is nearly always flat, I'm afraid."

The mice carried on mousing around, so presumably they didn't think that this was a major problem.

"So," said Betsy.

So, said forty-four noses.

So, said the single shaft of light, hovering expectantly over the piano.

So, So, So, ticked the grandfather clock.

"All right, all right," said Betsy. And she set the case down on the sounding board, opened the door, and said, "Play."

Forty-four reddish-brown streaks shot out of the case and into the guts of the piano.

They were so fast that she had to double-check that the case was empty to make sure she hadn't imagined it. It was. She picked it up and tucked it out of the way, under the stool.

"Ahem," she said. "Er. Mice. Chopin's Mazurka in B flat. Please."

And the mice began to play.

They played like a dawn chorus. They played like dappled sunlight. They played like the twinkling of stars. They played like forty-four delicate, tiny mice, scurrying around the very heart of the piano.

Betsy sank on to the stool. Now she understood how the Mazurka should sound. This was nothing like the tune she had played at the party. This was something else. This was magical.

"You're so good," she whispered as the

mice raced over the notes. "So good. But I can't use you. It would be cheating."

The mice trilled a particularly heavenly trill, because they didn't care a fig who was using them for what, as long as they were making music. Just then, Betsy heard someone walking along the landing. Someone in heels. A puzzled voice curled around the door: "Bertie, darling? I wasn't expecting you back so soon!"

Bella was home early.

Betsy opened her mouth to say, *No, it's me, with the most AMAZING mice.* But then she shut it again, because she had given her word to Gloria Sprightly not to tell anyone about the Method. She opened it a second time, because she knew she had to say something. But nothing came out and for two seconds she had a brief but very intense panic.

What on earth could she say?

In the meantime, the mice triumphantly thundered the Mazurka to a close, unaware of the trouble they were causing.

Bella opened the door. She stared. She swayed. She said, "Betsy?"

"Hi, Mum," said Betsy. Which didn't really solve anything.

"Darling!" cried her mother. She was swaying around with so much aplomb that Betsy was worried she might sway herself right over. "That was you? Why ... but I... Oh! It sounded WONDERFUL!"

Betsy swallowed. "Thanks."

"I had no idea," breathed Bella. "No idea that you could play like that."

"I get nervous," Betsy heard herself say.

Her voice seemed to have taken over – her brain was still panicking. "I can't play in front of other people. Especially," added her voice firmly, "if they watch my hands."

"Oh, that's very normal, Betsy darling, very normal. We all get nervous. I simply can't eat before a concert. And your father won't play for friends, not even me, it throws him off so much. And your grandfather always does concerts blindfolded so that he can pretend no one's there. And..." Betsy let the catalogue of nervous pianists wash over her, and she let Bella hug her and pat her and smooth her hair. She let it all happen and felt miserable. Inches away, forty-four mice stayed perfectly still. "Oh goodness, and we really thought you just weren't ... and of course it wasn't really important, but..." Bella pulled out a lace handkerchief and dabbed at her eyes. "Well," she said. "Never mind all that. It doesn't matter now. I'm so excited, Betsy, how wonderful."

It was as if a tap had been turned on. Bella talked and sobbed and swayed around for what seemed like hours. Betsy had never seen her so happy. She was enormously relieved when the phone rang and her mother finally left the room with a parting sob.

Betsy grabbed the carry case. "Home," she hissed to the mice. "Quickly." They shot in, and she zoomed up to the top floor, picked up the tank from the landing, hid the lot in her wardrobe, zoomed back to the morning room, and sat down to wait for Bella. She tried to look like someone who had just played a Mazurka, and not like someone with forty-four stupendously well-trained African pygmy mice in their wardrobe.

The expectant shaft of light had moved off the piano and was hiding itself awkwardly in a corner.

So, said the grandfather clock severely. *SO*.

"So!" said Bella, bursting back into the room. She beamed. "Time to celebrate!"

CHAPTER SIX

A Real Pianist

Bella's Celebration involved buying a lot of fancy cream cakes from the bakery down the road (which were excellent) and making a lot of tearful speeches (which were terrible). Then Grandad came in from the garden, and when he could make sense of what Bella was trying to say, he squeezed Betsy's shoulder and said, "Sounds lovely, B," (which was worst of all).

Bertram was the last to arrive. The news of

Betsy's hidden talent turned him a pleased sort of pink. Then he opened the box of cream cakes and found that they had all been eaten, and he looked just a tad less pink. He pushed his glasses up his nose forlornly.

"Betsy darling, you must play for your father," said Bella, for the twentieth time. "I can't begin to describe it. She's inherited your light touch, Bertie."

Bertram's beard twitched, which might have been gladness about the light touch, or might have been disappointment about the lack of cream cakes.

"Mum," said Betsy, "I'm not feeling great. Too much cake, I think." This was not, as it happened, a lie, but really her conscience was the bigger problem. She felt much too hot, and she couldn't think straight any more. "Can I be excused?"

So Betsy was duly excused and she went straight to bed, but she didn't sleep. She lay awake listening to her belly complain about the cream cakes and her conscience complain about the mice, and she waited to hear the sounds of everyone else going to bed. It was a very long wait. At last she heard them getting ready and bedroom doors shutting.

She waited a little longer, to be sure they were asleep. Then she switched on her lamp.

She took out Gloria's letters, and found the Instructions for Keeping Forty-Four Stupendously Well-Trained Pygmy Mice (with Full-Colour Illustrations). Inside the tank were water dishes and food dishes, and bags full of bedding and budgie seed, and lots of very small tunnels. Apparently, if you are a rodent, it is crazy-good fun to spend time in tunnels. Betsy set it all up according to the instructions and released the mice from their carry case into the tank.

It was hard to regret them quite so much, there in the lamplight. They were beautiful. Their fur was reddish-brown on top, but white on their bellies, and their eyes were bright and intelligent. They skittered about the tank as if they thought it was just as magnificent as the piano. Every now and then one would stop and blink up at her through the glass in a pleased sort of way – as if she didn't look like a Disappointment to them.

"It's all very well being cute," Betsy whispered, "but you've still caused a lot of trouble, mice."

Forty-four faces entirely failed to look ashamed.

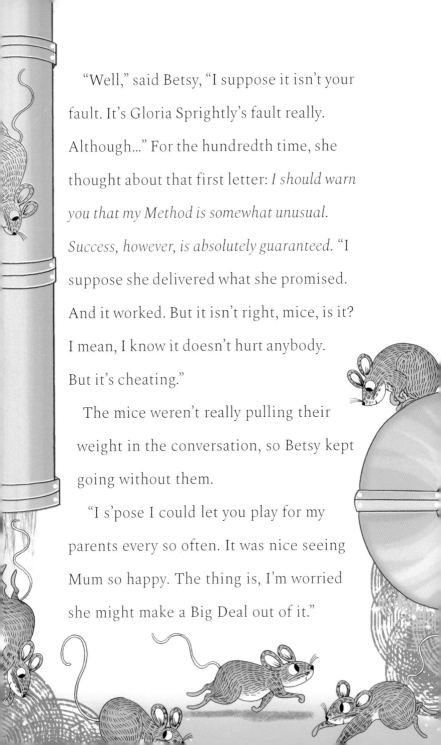

"Well," said Betsy, "I suppose it isn't your fault. It's Gloria Sprightly's fault really. Although…" For the hundredth time, she thought about that first letter: *I should warn you that my Method is somewhat unusual. Success, however, is absolutely guaranteed.* "I suppose she delivered what she promised. And it worked. But it isn't right, mice, is it? I mean, I know it doesn't hurt anybody. But it's cheating."

The mice weren't really pulling their weight in the conversation, so Betsy kept going without them.

"I s'pose I could let you play for my parents every so often. It was nice seeing Mum so happy. The thing is, I'm worried she might make a Big Deal out of it."

This was, of course, a bit like worrying that the British might make a Big Deal out of tea.

The next morning, two delivery men arrived with a van full of Something for Miss Betsy Bow-Linnet. For one wild moment, Betsy thought that Gloria had got overexcited and sent her a lifetime's supply of African pygmy mice. But the delivery was from Bella.

"It's from all of us," said Bella, squeezing Bertram's arm and swaying in Grandad's general direction.

"Indeed," said Bertram politely.

"What are you talking about?" said Grandad, less politely.

As the delivery men wheeled the Something into the house, Betsy's heart sank.

There was no doubt what it was. A baby grand piano is very hard to disguise, even if you have wrapped it in sparkling gold paper and put a massive bow on it. The piano inside was a glowing chestnut colour, with 'BBL' picked out in gold leaf on the lid.

"Where d'you want it?" asked the first delivery man.

Bella suggested Betsy's bedroom. Betsy wasn't very happy about that but the delivery men were definitely the least happy.

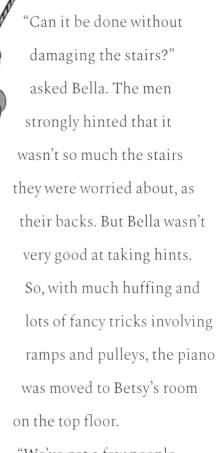

"Can it be done without damaging the stairs?" asked Bella. The men strongly hinted that it wasn't so much the stairs they were worried about, as their backs. But Bella wasn't very good at taking hints. So, with much huffing and lots of fancy tricks involving ramps and pulleys, the piano was moved to Betsy's room on the top floor.

"We've got a few people coming for coffee this afternoon," said Bella to Betsy. "Why don't you have a little play? Something nice for you to do while we're being boring."

'A few people', it turned out, meant 'everyone who's anyone in London, and all their friends and relations'. They came in an endless parade: no sooner had one platoon left than the doorbell rang for the next. And of course 'have a little play' meant 'let them hear your great and glorious genius'. Betsy knew that letting everyone hear the mice would blow the lie up out of control. But now that the lie had begun, it was already too late. She couldn't let her mother down.

"I don't care about that lot anyway," she told the mice, as they swarmed around inside her new baby grand. "They can believe what they like. Chopin's Mazurka in B flat, please." And the mice delighted the ears of everyone-

who's-anyone, while
Betsy read a book in
bed, and tried not to
feel too guilty.

A lot of people wanted
to come up and tell her how
marvellous she was, so she had
to be ready to scramble to the stool as soon
as there was a knock on the door. Even Vera
Brick said, "She is sounding better, Bella
dear," while looking crossly at the rug just to
Betsy's right. None of the people who came
upstairs seemed to be called Gloria.

By the end of the day, Betsy was thoroughly
sick of the Mazurka. "No offence," she said
to the mice, as she put them back in the tank.
"But if I have to listen to you play that piece
one more time, I might smash the piano apart

with my bare hands." This *was* quite offensive.
But the mice were very gracious about it.
"Anyway, that's that over. Well done ... and
thank you," she said, counting out forty-four
pumpkin seeds into the palm of her hand.

But of course, it wasn't over. Since the news
had got out about Betsy's talent, everyone-
who's-anyone had been planning a hundred
different glittering futures for Betsy over
their coffee and cake. And one of the last
people to arrive had a particularly pressing
proposal. After everyone else had left, Betsy
was called down to talk to him with her
mother.

"Betsy," said Bella. "This is Mr Anton
D'Lishus. He wants to tell you in person how
much he enjoyed your playing."

Betsy already knew all about Anton

D'Lishus. He was fabulously important and fabulously moustached. It wasn't clear exactly what he did, but he was Wealthy and Influential, and that seemed to be all anyone was interested in.

Anton praised Betsy's playing for an uncomfortably long time. Then he straightened the ends of his sleeves and twirled the ends of his moustache and got to business.

"Tomorrow night," he said, "I am hosting a charity gala concert at the Royal Albert Hall. You know the Hall well, of course?" Betsy did. It was a beautiful round

concert hall, one of the grandest in London. "Unfortunately," Anton went on, pressing his fingertips together delicately, "a small difficulty has arisen. The concert was supposed to be concluded by an alpine horn trio, but they have had to cancel, most unexpectedly."

"Oh dear," Bella said.

"On the contrary, my dear lady," he replied. "Oh hurrah. They sounded like a herd of highland cattle being run over by a slow-moving heavy goods vehicle. I was only having them as a favour to a very dear friend."

"Oh," said Bella.

So there was a gap in the programme. "And you would be just the ticket, Betsy," he said. "Simply tickety-boo. Both your parents have performed at the Hall, of course, and your grandfather too in his day. I'd be delighted to have you. I'd be honoured to have you." This is what his mouth said. His eyes said, *I'd be enormously relieved to have anyone at all, at such short notice.*

"Oh, Betsy would love that," cried Bella. "Wouldn't you, Betsy?"

"Hnngh," said Betsy.

"Splendid," said Anton D'Lishus. "I will see you there tomorrow then! Call-time is six o'clock."

"Hnnnnghgh," said Betsy. But the extra *nngh* didn't seem to help anyone understand what *Hnngh* meant. Before Betsy could explain, Anton D'Lishus was raising his hat to her and twirling his moustache in farewell. He left in the high spirits of a man who has lost an alpine horn trio and gained a Mazurka.

"Darling," said Bella, when he had gone, "I know you get nervous, but really, the only way to get more confident is to practise. That's how your father got his confidence. And this will be such a perfect opportunity – you can play the piece you know so well, and at a nice gala concert – and the Royal Albert Hall is lovely. I really think it will do you so much good. Once you've tried it, you can start enjoying it."

There was a feverish excitement in Bella's eyes. Betsy realized, with a sinking heart, that there was no point trying to persuade her that this might not be true.

She tried talking to her father about it instead. He was in the kitchen, stacking a colony of coffee cups into the dishwasher. "Dad," she said. "Anton D'Lishus has put me in his concert at the Royal Albert Hall tomorrow night."

"Splendid," said Bertram carefully, looking at Betsy over the top of his spectacles and waiting to find out whether it *was* splendid.

"I don't want to do it."

"I see," said Bertram. "So, er ... why *are* you doing it?"

Betsy shrugged. "Mum's so excited."

"Ah," said Bertram. "Yes. Yes, I can imagine that. Well, it's not so bad, B. It's a lovely big hall, so everyone's very far away. You can't see them, and they can hardly see you. It feels like there's no one else there at all."

"But I'll still know that there are people," said Betsy. "Thousands of people."

"Yes," said Bertram. "I suppose so." And this excellently true point flummoxed him, so that was the end of his advice. He looked at her with kind concern, but this only got them so far. To fill the pause, he said, "5,272 people to be exact. If they've sold all the seats."

Betsy thanked him, and hastily left to find Grandad.

Grandad was in the parlour. When Betsy told him the problem his elbows wafted around in concern, and he said, "But aren't you pleased, B? I thought you wanted to be a *Real Pianist*?"

"Yes..." said Betsy.

"B, it's just a bit of fun. Remember that, and enjoy it. And you'll be able to prove that vile *Natter* wrong in front of all those people!"

This was true. Betsy nodded.

"So," said Grandad, "What's wrong, B?"

She paused, almost resolving to tell him. The pause outstayed its welcome. Then she said, "Oh dear – sorry, Grandad, the ferns are giving me the worst hay fever," and skedaddled before the pause could get any longer.

Then there was no one left to talk to

except the mice.

"Well," she said, "I imagine we'll get away with it. No one will see my hands in a hall that size, with the piano angled away. But now I'm lying to 5,272 people at once."

The mice were magnificently unconcerned by this. *Why,* their busy tails seemed to say, *should we waste time worrying about it, when we all know you're going to have to do it anyway?*

Betsy sighed. "I'm a bit scared, mice."

One little mouse paused to look at her, nose in the air, whiskers most unbendingly stern. And it seemed to Betsy to be saying: *May I remind you, B, that Miss Betsy Bow-Linnet is no coward.*

"Oh all right, fine," she said. "Fine. Whatever. But it's going to be awful." The thought of all those thousands of people was making her feel worse than the cream cakes. Not only thousands of strangers, but all her family, and the inevitable Vera Brick, and the so-impressive Anton D'Lishus with his moustache, and ... then a thought struck her.

"I wonder if Gloria Sprightly will be there?"

CHAPTER SEVEN

The Royal Albert Hall

The next day Betsy hid in her room, letting the mice play to demonstrate that she was 'practising'. As they tinkled, she paced up and down, trying to decide what to do for the best. Countless times she put her hand on the door knob, resolving to tell her family everything. But then she remembered her mother's overjoyed face, and her own promise to Gloria Sprightly, and her hand fell again.

Bella made macaroni cheese for lunch,

which was Betsy's favourite, and she told her not to be nervous, and that she was very proud. Which just made Betsy feel worse.

"Anton D'Lishus called," Bella said. "And he's managed to get the best seats in the house for me and Dad and Grandad. So we can all have a really special night to remember. Isn't that lovely?"

It was one of the least lovely things Betsy had ever heard. She was willing to bet that hearing Anton D'Lishus's alpine horn trio would be lovelier.

Grandad walked her to the Royal Albert Hall for six o'clock sharp. When Betsy had been there for concerts, she would enter through the glass double doors, where everything is cheerfully lit and colourful, and people in waistcoats buzz around being helpful with merry aplomb, and you are altogether encouraged to have a Nice Time.

Today, Betsy and Grandad didn't go in through the have-a-nice-time doors. They went through a small, dark-wood door to the right, marked 'stage door'. The room behind was mushroom-coloured and small. They queued up at the desk, behind a man in an astonishing hat.

"Grandad," whispered Betsy. "I feel a bit sick."

"Now now, B," said Grandad. "No kicking the piano, and no being sick on stage. Somebody has to clean that floor, young lady."

"But Grandad—"

But just then the astonishing hat moved away with the man underneath it, and the woman at the desk was saying, "Name?" Her name was SANDRA, according to her badge.

"Betsy Bow-Linnet," said Betsy Bow-Linnet. "And this is my grandad." Grandad's elbows billowed in greeting.

Sandra paid no attention to Grandad's elbows. She was scanning the concert schedule. "You're not on my list," she said. "I can't let you in if you're not on the list."

"Oh no," said Betsy, unconvincingly.

"She's the last act of the night," said Grandad. "It was arranged yesterday."

Sandra consulted the list. "Says here that the last act is an alpine horn trio." She peered at Betsy's bag, as if she was wondering whether it could hold three alpine horns and two more people. It was a large bag – Betsy had borrowed her father's big leather one, to hide the mice's case – but it wasn't *that* big.

"Well," sighed Sandra, world-weary. "I'll ask."

Grandad and Betsy took a seat, while Sandra muttered to someone through a walkie-talkie. Eventually she looked up and had a go at smiling. "OK, Betsy, everything's sorted. Someone will be down to meet you."

She turned the smile-thing to Grandad. "Thanks for bringing her," she said, in a voice that meant *You can leave now.*

Grandad squeezed Betsy's shoulder. "Now remember, you have nothing at all to be nervous about. Betsy Bow-Linnet will not be intimidated by a lot of velvet and pomp. Have fun, B!" And with that, he flapped his way back outside, and left Betsy to wait in the mushroom room with Sandra and forty-four mice.

A young woman called Florence met Betsy and took her backstage. She had a smart black suit and a smart blonde bob, and she was very friendly. She got Betsy some lemonade and introduced her to some of the people backstage, and told her what was going to happen.

"There'll be a soundcheck soon," she said. "Which is when we make sure that the tech is ready to go. It will only take a mo."

The soundcheck took the longest mo known to man. Everyone had to mill around waiting to troop on stage and poke the piano or toot a trumpet or whatever, and then troop back off again, while people said "One-two" into microphones and the lights did dizzy things up above them. Everyone seemed to know each other, and no one talked to Betsy. She clutched her leather bag and prayed that they would all go soon so that she could release the mice into the piano.

The longer it dragged on, the more fervently she prayed. She began to worry that they would all still be faffing around when the audience came in. But at last, the sound had been thoroughly checked and everyone was ordered backstage again.

Betsy lingered behind, pretending to tie a shoelace. As soon as the coast was clear she pattered across the huge stage to the piano and opened the case. "Play!" she whispered.

Forty-four pygmy mice took their place on one of the most famous stages in the world. Betsy Bow-Linnet left them to wait and took her place in the green room of one of the most famous stages in the world. Her heartbeat took its place in her throat and doubled its speed. Everything was ready. And not a moment too soon.

The backstage room at the Albert Hall is right below the stage itself. She could hear the audience. They were a thunderstorm of polite chitchat. Then she heard the storm go quiet, and the concert began. As she was on last, she had to listen to the whole thing, which went like this:

- Mr D'Lishus made a speech
- The Queen's Second-Best Orchestra played Something Jolly
- The Queen's Second-Best Orchestra took a really long time getting off stage
- Mr D'Lishus made a speech
- A woman sang in Italian about having three dead husbands and a sick parakeet
- Mr D'Lishus read a poem
- A trumpet proved just how loud

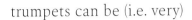

trumpets can be (i.e. very)

- Mr D'Lishus gave a short lecture on moustaches

- The Queen's Second-Best Orchestra took a really long time getting back on stage, played Something Showy, then spent an unbelievably long time getting off stage again

- A man told everyone about the charity that the gala was raising money for. He was quickly replaced by Mr D'Lishus.

- Bagpipes happened. Children cried.

That was Betsy's cue. She got up to walk to the wings. She wished Grandad was there. Or Florence. The stage manager was very stern and didn't smile at all.

"Magnificent!" Anton D'Lishus was saying, with a flourish of his moustache.

"Let's have one more round of applause for the International Calamity of Bagpipes!" 5,272 people applauded politely. "Ticketyboo! Now, ladies and gentlemen, we have something very special indeed for you before you go home tonight. This talented young lady is here to make her debut!"

Betsy peeked out. The stage was a blaze of light. Beyond that was total darkness.

"Gracing us with her astonishing pianoplaying for the Very First Time, please welcome to the stage ... Betsy Bow-Linnet!"

"Cue," said the stage manager, in case Betsy had missed it. For a moment, Betsy couldn't remember whether or not Betsy Bow-Linnet was a coward. She had a feeling that she probably wasn't. So she stepped out on to the stage.

5,272 people thundered their applause. Betsy trekked across the stage through the dazzling lights. She concentrated very carefully on breathing and tried to ignore the hammering of her heart. At last she arrived at the piano, sat down, put her hands on the keys, and murmured very quietly, "Chopin's Mazurka in B flat."

Nothing happened.

She cleared her throat, and said more loudly, "Chopin's Mazurka in B flat."

There was a polite smattering of applause from the front rows – no one else could hear her. Including, it seemed, the mice.

Betsy's mind raced. She had definitely put them in there. What was going on?

Then the awful, heavy, clunking penny dropped, right into her gut. *We have something very special for you all, before you go home tonight.*

Anton D'Lishus had said *home.*

The mice were gone.

CHAPTER EIGHT

Night

For a second, Betsy just looked blankly at her hands. The second seemed to last a very, very long time. In the darkness, someone coughed.

After that, everything happened very fast indeed.

First, there was a shriek from the front row. It sounded so much like a very loud doorbell that Florence, who was patrolling outside, looked puzzled and called up front of house on her walkie-talkie. But Betsy

knew at once that it was Vera Brick.

Vera shrieked again for good measure and

shouted, "MOUSE! There's a MOUSE! Oh,

it's climbing in my hair!"

This caused a lot more shrieking from the seats nearby, and climbing on to chairs, and wailing and general idiotic flapping about.

One or two people had actually seen a mouse, but most were getting hysterical just in case. Vera was still trying to shake the first mouse out of her perm, where it had found a particularly comfortable curl.

Up in the circle and the gallery, nobody could make out what all the shrieking was about but they guessed it must be pretty bad. Rumours started to fly: there's a fire. The roof's caving in. The bagpipes are coming back. Like a great wave, the shrieking and the panic spread through the Hall. People began to push for the doors.

5,272 seats suddenly appeared out of the darkness as the lights went up. Ushers hurried in to try and calm people down, but people were not interested in being calm. Florence had appeared at the side of the stage, smile gone, walkie-talkie warbling furiously. Mr D'Lishus followed her and was bellowing, "Ladies and gentlemen! Ladies and gentlemen, PLEASE!" but everyone was enjoying the scandal far too much to listen.

While everyone-who's-anyone in London panicked over the world's smallest mice,

Betsy Bow-Linnet left the piano and slipped backstage. Nobody noticed.

Backstage, word had spread, and everyone was joining in the general panic. The bagpipers were shaking imaginary mice out of their pipes, the opera singer was beating the ground with a broom, and the conductor of the orchestra was weeping hysterically. Nobody looked at Betsy as she slipped into her seat and thought furiously.

She trusted the mice to look after themselves – they could scurry away from trouble with lightning speed, and it is easy enough to hide when you are one inch long. But then what? They couldn't be left here. She had to get them back. She tried to come up with a plan.

Grandad would walk straight home, while Bella and Bertram would stay for endless drinks with endless friends. It should be simple enough to trick them all into thinking she was being taken home by someone else. And then – but she didn't want to think about 'and then', because that led to hundreds of other 'and then's, on and on and on. She had to go one step at a time.

Picking up Bertram's large bag with the hidden case, she weaved through the confusion of musicians, out into the Hall, and went to find Grandad. She saw him before he saw her. He was waiting in the foyer, looking out for her anxiously – but as usual, he hid away all the anxiety as soon as he spotted her and smiled cheerfully.

"Well," said Grandad. "Quite a show, eh? Sorry you didn't get to play, B."

"I don't mind," said Betsy.

"I suppose you'll want to stay for the hoo-ha with your parents?" Grandad asked. (Hoo-ha was the word Grandad used for anything that involved talking to people.)

"I think so," said Betsy. "I'll see you at home."

"Right you are. Well if it all gets a bit much here, give me a call and I can come and rescue you. And may I say, B, that you walked on to the stage magnificently."

Betsy forced a laugh. "Thanks, Grandad."

Next, Betsy found her parents, surrounded by friends at the bar.

"Darling!" Bella scooped her up in a hug. "You must be so disappointed! But you mustn't be upset. Mr D'Lishus says you can play again soon."

"Great," said Betsy.

Her father held out a flower. "They wouldn't let me backstage," he explained. "I brought this for your hair." He tucked it in place. "Beautiful, B. Are you OK?"

He looked at her so kindly that Betsy longed to tell him everything. Her eyes stung. "Fine thanks. I'm a bit tired. Is it all right if I go home with Grandad?"

"Of course, darling!" said Bella. "It's been quite a day! I do hope you're not too sad about it. If you're still awake when I get back I'll bring up some cocoa."

"I'll definitely be asleep," said Betsy hastily. "Don't worry about coming to see me."

Once she had passed her parents back to the hoo-ha, Betsy snuck upstairs – and when at last there was a quiet moment, she found herself somewhere to hide. A door on the first floor turned out to be a cleaning cupboard, blissfully quiet and dark. Betsy sank inside, hugged the bag to her chest – and waited.

The thing
about cupboards is
that they are the same
everywhere. Hiding in a
cupboard in the splendour
of the Royal Albert Hall is
not so different from hiding
in a cupboard in a school
hall or your aunt Mildred's
house. There was a lot of dust,
and a moppish-shaped thing,

and a large hooverish thing, and a crack of light where the cupboard doors met. Betsy breathed in the dusty smell and it smelled like every game of hide-and-seek she had ever played.

She squatted there for what felt like hours. At last, the crack of light was switched off. Footsteps faded away and a distant door shut. Betsy was left with the enormous silence of 5,272 people who had gone home and left her behind.

She opened the cupboard door. Dim footlights had been left on, illuminating the tiled edges of the corridor, and very little else. Squinting at the signs, she followed the arrows pointing to the stalls and entered the red velvet belly of the Hall. In here, as outside in the corridor, the footlights were her only guide. Most of the seats were lost in the darkness.

She put down the case and opened the catch. "Home?" she tried – without much hope.
The mice could be anywhere by now, and she needed to be close enough for them to hear her. No red streaks appeared. She was going to have to do this the long way. "All right," she said. "Have it your way. We've got all night."
And she set out to find forty-four one-inch mice in the enormous Hall, one seat at a time.

Have you ever worked all through the night, alone? It is miserable. Time lollops along strangely, sometimes racing and sometimes standing perfectly still, and you have nothing but your own thoughts for company. Betsy was trying to avoid her thoughts, because they were inconvenient things like *What if I don't find them all?* and *What if I DO find them all? There will be another show, and another. Am I going to have to keep doing concerts for my whole life now, and lying to more and more people?* and *Oh help.* So she just concentrated on the task at hand, one mouse at a time. G-to-G-sharp-fourth-octave was curled up on seat C32. B-to-C-seventh-octave was nibbling a curtain in the second box. Every time Betsy found one, she showed it the case, and it whisked happily into its compartment.

By midnight, she had ten mice. By 2 a.m., she had fifteen. She found a whole nest in the Upper Circle and brought it up to thirty-two by 3 a.m. By five o'clock,

she had forty-three mice. It
must have been dawn outside
but in the Hall it was the same
relentless red.

By six, she still had forty-three.
She kicked a velvet seat. These,
she had discovered, are the perfect
thing to kick.

"I hate stupid mice and I hate Gloria stupid Sprightly," she announced. *And I hate my mum*, thought a corner of her brain. The rest of her brain looked at the thought in surprise. Where did that come from? But the thought had vanished again. She didn't really hate her mum, of course – but she was very, very tired of trying so hard to make her happy.

Before she could decide whether to kick the chair again or try screaming, a figure appeared in a box above her. She froze. They looked at each other.

The figure coughed, a sheepish *ahem*. "Have you found them all yet?" it asked.

Betsy blinked up at the box. No matter how much she blinked, he was still there.

"Dad?"

CHAPTER NINE

Dawn

Her father peered down at her. His pyjama trousers poked out below his long coat, and his concern peeked out from behind his beard.

"Hello, B," he said. "I'm sorry I didn't come sooner. Your grandad took forever to go to bed."

This did not answer any of the most important questions, and Bertram knew it. He hid behind his beard more than ever.

"Look, let's finish here," he said. "Then I'll

explain, I promise. How many are left?"

"Just one," said Betsy. "F-to-F-sharp-fourth-octave."

"Righto," said Bertram – and he got on his knees and began to make little squeaky noises, shuffling along a row of seats. Betsy automatically scanned the nearest chairs, but she wasn't really looking. What was going on? Surely her father wasn't Gloria Sprightly?

And before she could get her thoughts into any sort of order, suddenly, there he was – F-to-F-sharp, whisking along the velvet back of a chair. Betsy only just pulled herself together in time. "Home!" she called, raising the box frantically. "Hey! Home!"

Just in time. With F-to-F-sharp curled up happily inside, it was finally over.

"Got it!" Betsy called. "Dad?"

Bertram's head appeared over the top of a chair. "Oh well done, B. Shall we get some breakfast?" His eyes lit up. "How about cream cakes?"

"Sure," said Betsy, "But—"

"I'll explain, B, I promise," he said. "Breakfast. Then explanations." And he looked so pale and tired that Betsy didn't argue. She slipped one hand in his, her other hand clutching the leather bag: and Bertram Bow-Linnet, Betsy Bow-Linnet and forty-four African pygmy mice left the Royal Albert Hall.

Outside, it was quiet. The light was still weak, and the air was chilly. Bertram led the way, with the confident step of a man who knows, without hesitation, where you can find cream cakes at the crack of dawn in Kensington.

They stopped at a small cafe with a peeling blue front, where some fresh eclairs were at that moment being placed in the window. A bell tinkled as they stepped inside. They were the only customers.

"Right," said Bertram, when they were seated and had ordered two of the eclairs. "Right, right, right." There was an expectant sort of pause, and then he said, "Right," again.

"Dad," said Betsy. "Are you Gloria Sprightly?"

Bertram's eyebrows shot away from each other in surprise. "Goodness me, no! Is that what you thought? I suppose ... yes, I see ... well." He rubbed his beard anxiously. "No, Betsy, I'm not Gloria Sprightly. But I wish I knew who she was. She's been sending me African pygmy mice for seventeen years."

"What?" said Betsy. "You mean... Can't you play?"

"Oh, a bit. Not enough," he said. He sighed, and then he began his story, addressing most of it to the eclair for courage. "I met your mother at a party full of pianists. I'd ended up there through a friend of a friend of a friend, and your mother just assumed I was a pianist too, and I'd had a bit of sherry, and I wasn't quite thinking straight..." He rubbed his beard nervously. "It wasn't meant to be a lie, B. I know how to play the piano. I'd played a bit, as a boy. But by the time I realized how important it was to her that I really played, I had also realized that I could never love any other woman as madly as I loved her.

"I tried the honest way. I bought a little

upright piano for my flat and I practised every hour of every day. I practised so much that all the neighbours tried to have me thrown out. And then one day I finally played for her, and she just broke down in tears and ran out of my flat.

"That was when I first heard from Gloria. I bought some pumpkin seeds, and … well, you know the rest. I told Bella that I was normally much better – that I suffered terribly from nerves, especially when I'm watched. And I let the mice play for her. It was terribly dishonest of me, of course, but – well – you understand, don't you, B? You used them too. As soon as I heard them playing your new baby grand, I knew."

"But I didn't mean to," said Betsy, a little harshly. She didn't mean to be unkind: she was too tired to think straight and the truth just oozed out of her like cream out of an eclair. "It was an accident. She heard them and I didn't know what else to say."

"Oh," said Bertram, forlorn, a little touch of cream in his beard. "Ah." And for a moment, neither of them spoke.

It was Betsy who broke the silence. "And Mum has never found out, in all those years?"

Bertram shook his head. "I refuse to play for her alone, or for friends," he said. "I just blame the nerves." And Betsy remembered her mother telling her this – accepting it, without question. She felt awful about all the lies and it must have shown on her face, because Bertram drooped more than ever. "Oh dear, B," he said. "I'm so sorry. I've almost told her, so many times. But the lie kept growing and growing, and now I'm too afraid..." His beard quivered. "Every day, B, I wish more than anything that I had never even seen those mice. Truly I do."

Betsy couldn't stand to see him so sad. "It's all right," she said – although that wasn't quite true. "I get it," she said – and that was true.

He patted her hand gratefully. Neither of them could think of anything to say. "We should get back, B," said Bertram at last. "Before your mother wakes up."

Sneaking around. Secret eclairs while Bella slept, sleepless nights in concert halls, stealing moments alone with the mice. Betsy didn't want any of it. She wanted to rewind to a time when she didn't have any secrets, and her father was honest and dependable, and her mother loved them both without worrying about silly things like piano-playing.

But she couldn't. So she stood up, put her hand in her father's, and walked home through London as it slowly woke up.

Home was quiet. The ferns whispered secrets to each other as Betsy and Bertram pushed through them. "I'd best go back to bed, B," said Bertram. "You know – for appearances."

"Right," said Betsy. "What happens next, Dad?"

"I'm not sure," said Bertram sadly. "Can we talk about it when we've had some sleep, B?"

And Betsy didn't know either, so she agreed.

She was exhausted, but she knew that she wouldn't be able to sleep. When she had put the mice back in the wardrobe, she wandered the house, breathing in the comforting smell of ferns and trying not to think too hard about anything.

She didn't plan where to wander, but her

feet seemed to have it under control. They took her to Bertram's piano ("She's inherited your light touch, Bertie"), then they took her up to the morning room on the first floor, to the broken piano where she had first heard the mice, then they took her up to the second floor, to the family photos lined up in Grandad's study. Grandad and a small Bella, a young Bella and Bertram, Bella and Bertram plus a tiny Betsy. And the only photo of Grandma in the house, a photo of her with Grandad, sitting in a silver frame on Grandad's old-fashioned writing desk. Betsy had always thought that she looked nice. Her hair was unruly like her granddaughter's, and Bella had her curling smile. She wore a glittering, high-collared jacket, something she must have kept from her circus days.

Next to the photo was a key that Betsy had
never seen before. She picked it up: it was
silver too, and heavy. It looked like it must be
for the desk's drawers. She tried them all with
no luck, until she got to the large drawer at the
bottom, which slid open with a sigh.

"Oh, Grandad," she said softly.

The framed photo was not the only picture of
Grandma in the house. Grandad had everything
here. Photos from their life together, and
letters, and posters from all her shows, and

newspaper clippings. There was even a box
containing a beautiful velvet cloak, which
Grandma must have worn to perform.

Betsy shut the box carefully and picked up
a newspaper clipping from the top of the pile.
It showed a very elderly Grandma, with the
same curly smile, and curly wrinkles to match.
It was an obituary from the *Times*, celebrating
Grandma's life.

"Oh, Grandad," said Betsy. "You never said."
And she started to read:

BERYL O'KEEFE

A LIFE LESS ORDINARY

Few circus performers leave a legacy to match that of Beryl O'Keefe, who died peacefully last Tuesday while on tour with her spectacular animals. She was best known for her 'dozen dancing dogs', but she also trained horses, birds and even rabbits.

Her astonishing inventiveness has left a lasting mark on the circus arts. Performing under the stage name of Gloria Sprightly, Beryl will be remembered as...

Betsy caught up with herself a few words later, and rewound. Gloria Sprightly?

She sat down heavily at the desk and tried to think straight. She checked the date: the paper was three years old. True, she was enormously tired, and she could feel that this was making her a bit muddled – but she was still sure that there was no way that a ghost could send a box of African pygmy mice through the post.

She saw the flapping of an elbow out of the corner of her eye and jerked her head up guiltily. Grandad stood in the doorway. It was hard to tell if he was horribly angry, or horribly upset or doing an impression of a fish.

"Betsy," he said at last. "What are you doing?"

"Sorry, Grandad," said Betsy. "I just…"

And then she couldn't keep all the secrets inside her any longer: "Grandad, I've been getting letters from Gloria Sprightly. So has Dad."

Grandad was silent. His elbows went very still and his head flopped forwards. Then he sank into a chair opposite Betsy and sighed. His voice, when he spoke, was tired.

"I know."

CHAPTER TEN

Gloria Sprightly Again

"Perhaps the time has come," Grandad said, "to explain."

Betsy had already had one explanation for the day. She didn't especially want another one. But they were here now. That seemed to be the trouble lately – things got started before she had time to blink, and then she was stuck finishing them.

"OK," she said, hugging her knees up to her chest, and hoping it wasn't a difficult sort of explanation.

"Your grandma," said Grandad, "was the most brilliant animal trainer the circus world has ever seen."

"But she's—"

"Yes," agreed Grandad. "Oh, this is tricky, B. I had better begin at the beginning." He crumpled in on himself a bit, as if the beginning was his least favourite place. "When your grandma left us," he said, "your mother threw herself into her piano-playing. That had always been our thing – mine and Bella's – nothing to do with Beryl. So we clung to it. We played every day after school, just like we always had, just as if nothing had changed."

Betsy looked at the photo of a young Bella on Grandad's desk. She had never heard anything about her mother's childhood. She wished they could stop for a minute in this part of the story and talk about this young, different Bella. But Grandad was still marching forwards with his Explanation. Betsy got the impression that it was a relief for him to talk.

"I encouraged it at first, of course. She had talent and it made her happy. But after a while, I did start to worry that she seemed to have lost all faith in *people*. People couldn't be trusted, music could. That was the way she thought for years. She found it so hard to trust anyone, B, that she became really lonely. And then –" Grandad tapped the photo of Bella and Bertram – "then she met your father.

"Oh, B, she was so happy. I hadn't seen her that happy since she was a little girl. It seemed enormously good luck – that she had found someone she loved, who also happened to be a pianist. What were the odds? Except..." And Grandad trailed off, unsure what Betsy knew.

"Except that he's no good," said Betsy. "Like me."

Grandad shrugged sadly. "Not no good, Betsy. But not really musical. Your mother was torn apart. She loved him, but if he wasn't a pianist like us, she couldn't find it in herself to trust him. It was poppycock, of course, but it ran so deeply by then. Oh, she was miserable. Anyone who loved her, B, would have wanted to find a way to help her."

Betsy frowned. "So," she said, "her mum …
my grandma … sent the mice?"

"No, B. The name was just a fond touch
from a silly old man."

For a moment, Betsy couldn't understand
who the silly old man was. Then she realized
that she was looking at one. "You?"

Grandad's elbows quivered, in the elbowy
equivalent of a blush. "They were our project
– mine and your grandma's – an experiment
I came up with to try and keep her brilliant
mind busy. I never guessed that they would
come in so handy."

Betsy gaped at him.

"I'm sorry they caused such a fiasco at the
Hall," he said. "I was going to come and help
you once the guests had all gone, even if it
did blow my cover, but your father wouldn't

go to bed. It took me forever to realize he'd twigged about the mice, and *he* was waiting for *me* to go to bed too! But I promise, B," he said, "they normally work like a charm."

"But Grandad" said Betsy, finding her voice at last. "It's cheating!"

"Yes," said Grandad. "You're right, of course." And he was suddenly quite still, as if he had only just felt the full weight of this thought. "I just didn't want my Bella to push away the only friend she'd ever found," he said quietly. "You have no idea how lonely she was. And I did promise myself I wouldn't give them to you, but then that confounded *Natter* just made me so angry. I had been training a new set for Bertram in the garden shed – his are very old – so they were ready to go." He ventured a tiny smile. "And they are rather magnificent, aren't they?"

Betsy wanted to say that magnificence was not the point. But Grandad was looking at her so hopefully. She felt a wave of tiredness. Loving people and being disappointed by them at the same time was very hard work.

"They are, Grandad," she said. "Really. But I don't want them. I don't want to spend my whole life lying like Dad."

"Oh." Grandad considered this, head thrust forward, elbows still. "I didn't – I meant – I thought," he said, "that I was helping." Then for a long while he didn't speak. He stared straight ahead, wrestling with uncomfortable new thoughts.

Betsy found it too sad to look at him, so she looked instead at the smiling Bow-Linnets in the photographs. Young and old, Grandma and Grandad, Bella and Grandad, Bertram and Bella, Bertram and Bella and Betsy. All ages at once, all the twists and turns of their story flattened out and put neatly into frames.

"Maybe," said Grandad at last, "we will

have to unravel this from the beginning.
It's probably for the best." And his forehead
wrinkled with worry – like all the twists and
turns of their story folding back in again.

CHAPTER ELEVEN

Unravelling

First they talked to Bertram. They did it that afternoon, when Bella was out rehearsing.

When he learned who the real Gloria Sprightly was he went very pink behind his beard, and spluttered for quite a long time. The spluttering is difficult to translate. But if you have ever felt angry about something while knowing that you were also to blame, so that you didn't know whether to shout or cry or scream or what ... then you might know what he meant.

Then Grandad explained that they wanted to tell Bella the truth. This idea was such a relief that Bertram forgot all about shouting or screaming and he just settled for crying, until his nose was red and his beard was glistening. After that, he and Grandad were united, because they had to do the next bit together – and it was going to be hard.

While they waited for Bella to come home, Betsy met Bertram's mice, kept beneath a floorboard under his piano. They were his third set, but even so they were pretty old now, for mice. Eighty-eight weary eyes blinked up at her from their tank, much more battered than the matching tank in her bedroom cupboard.

Forty-four noses twitched a sleepy 'hello'.

"It will be nice for them to stop playing," said Bertram. "It's high time they retired." And the mice twitched in approval and snuggled down more comfortably into their bedding.

Just then, they heard footsteps in the hall. Bella was home. Instinctively Bertram returned the tank beneath the floorboard.

Grandad and Bertram explained things to Bella without Betsy. She crept out to her spot at the banisters on the top floor and stared at the parlour door, willing it to go well. So she was perfectly positioned to see the top of Bella's head as she marched out, slamming the front door behind her.

For a little while after that, Bella stayed away. Grandad's head folded up in more and more wrinkles each day, and Bertram hid further and further behind his beard, and everything seemed to just get worse. That is the trouble with secrets. To unpick them, you have to unravel everything else as well.

But then one morning there was the *click-clack* of a pair of high-heeled shoes on marble, and Bella was back. And from that day on, they started stitching things back together again.

Betsy never knew what Bella said to Bertram, or Grandad. She could only ever know what Bella said to her. She came into Betsy's room while she was playing with the mice on her bed.

"Sorry," said Betsy. "I was just—"

"Don't be," said Bella. "They are rather sweet, aren't they, darling?" And she sat on the edge of the bed and put out her hand to the nearest.

"Don't hold them," said Betsy. "If you hold them too tightly you might squash them."

Bella let one run on to the back of her hand. It blinked up at her innocently, like a good intention.

"Betsy," said Bella – and her mouth wasn't curling up now, not even a little bit – "Grandad told me what you heard. About being a disappointment…"

"Oh," said Betsy.

"Oh, darling," said Bella. She looked as though her hay fever was getting very bad indeed. "I'm so sorry. It's true I always hoped you'd love playing with us. Well, with me. And I was disappointed that you didn't. But you aren't a disappointment. You could never be."

Betsy felt a bit hay fevery herself. "I wish I *could* play with you though. Maybe if I practise…"

Bella curled herself around Betsy in an enormous hug before she could finish the sentence. "Don't," she said. "Don't waste your time on something you don't love. You are good and kind and brave and full of your own thoughts under all that hair. Which –" she pulled back and inspected – "you really must brush, darling. And I am so proud of you."

There was a sniff (from Betsy) and a squeak (from a mouse that had accidentally got stuck in the hug, and had to be released very quickly) and then just a peaceful sort of quiet as they lay back on the bed.

It was Betsy who broke it first. "Are you and Dad OK? And Grandad?"

She felt Bella nodding, a nudging against her shoulder. "Yes. It's complicated. Of course. What they did was wrong. But I love them and they love me, and I understand why they did what they did. We're going to be all right."

"That's good," said Betsy. "That's brilliant."

They lay quietly a little longer, and this time Bella broke the silence. "Betsy, I know I'm a bit ... silly, sometimes, about my music." She sighed. "And all the parties and things, they're a bit much. And I have some awful friends."

Betsy laughed a little at that. "I hate Vera Brick, Mum."

Bella giggled. "Oh, me too. Wasn't it great when a mouse got in her hair?"

Betsy's laugh bubbled up so unstoppably that she could only nod.

"I get swept up in it all sometimes," said Bella. "But I don't care about any of that lot – not really. You do know that I love you, don't you, darling?"

"I thought I was –" and Betsy flung her arms

out in exaggerated mockery of her mother –
"*a Terrible Disappointment*?"

"You," said her mother, "are a terrible tease. I don't sound like that."

"You do," said Betsy, nudging a mouse out of her mother's curls. "But I love you too."

The mouse from Bella's hair scurried on to Betsy's arm. "Do you want to see something cool?" she asked her mum, sitting up straight and holding the mouse aloft. "I thought I should teach them something else. Since they won't be playing the piano any more." She looked sternly at the rodent formerly known as F-to-F-sharp and whistled a low whistle. Very solemnly, the mouse stood up on his back legs, gave a little spin, and bowed.

Bella laughed in astonishment. "How did you make it do that?"

Betsy shrugged. This was a tricky question to answer. The hours had passed like a blur – hours Betsy had spent in her room, trying to forget that her mother was gone, convincing the mice to run through mazes, and reach up for pumpkin seeds, and run with ink on their paws over paper to leave pictures, and stand on their back legs and bow and spin and dance. It had all been so interesting and so obvious to her, she couldn't really explain exactly what she had done. "I just sort of ... tried things," she said. "Until they understood what I wanted them to do."

Bella was silent.

"Do you mind?" said Betsy. "We don't have to keep them if you don't want them."

"No, no, they're brilliant," said Bella. "I love them. It's just … you reminded me of someone."

There was a knock at the door and a chin appeared. Betsy blinked in confusion, before she realized with a start that it was her father back from a trip to the barbers and, most astonishingly, shaved. His face was moon-shaped and kind. She liked it – now you could see what he was thinking.

"Forgive the intrusion," said Bertram. "I was just wondering if anybody else wants some cream cakes?"

"I DO!" bellowed Grandad from his study across the landing.

"Oh, yes please, darling," said Bella.

Betsy laughed. "You've only been home five minutes, Dad! But yes please."

And at the sound of that word home, there was a flurry of reddish-brown all over Bella and Betsy and the bed, and forty-four truly astonishing African pygmy mice hurried back into their tank. They curled up like forty-four tiny ferns,

they shut their eighty-eight eyes,

and before you could say

'Gloria Sprightly' ...

they were asleep.

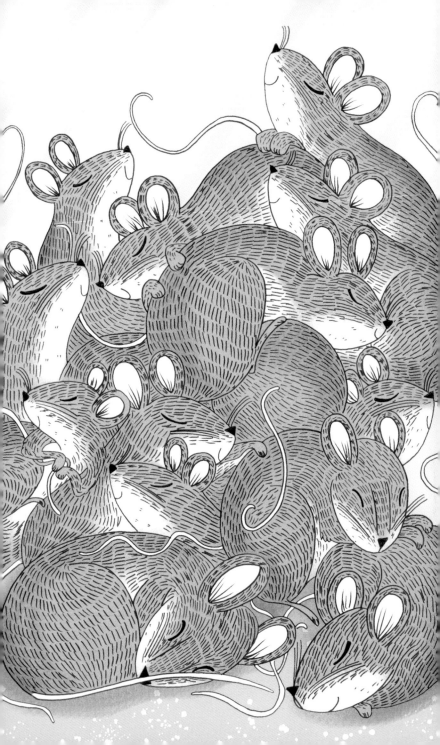

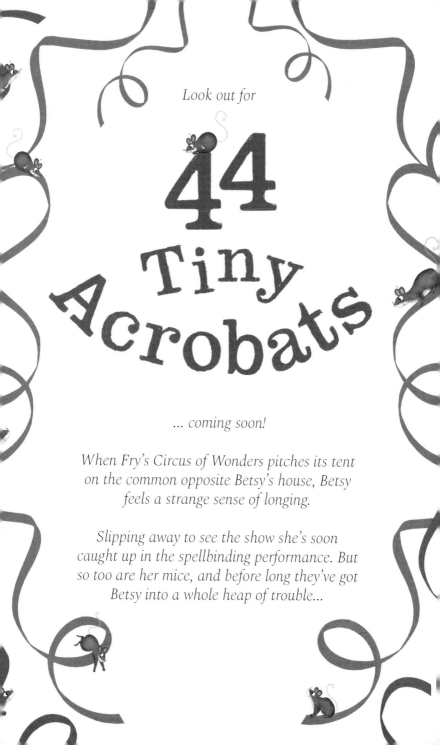

Look out for

44

Tiny
Acrobats

... coming soon!

When Fry's Circus of Wonders pitches its tent on the common opposite Betsy's house, Betsy feels a strange sense of longing.

Slipping away to see the show she's soon caught up in the spellbinding performance. But so too are her mice, and before long they've got Betsy into a whole heap of trouble...

ABOUT THE AUTHOR

Sylvia Bishop spent an entire childhood reading
fiction, dreaming up stories and pretending.
Now she writes her stories down for a living,
preferably by lamp-light with tea. Her first book,
Erica's Elephant, was published in 2016. She has
since written two further titles for young readers,
The Bookshop Girl and *A Sea of Stories*, and two
middle-grade mysteries, *The Secret of the Night
Train* and *Trouble in New York*. Her books
have been translated into sixteen languages,
including French, Dutch, Russian and Japanese.
Find out more at sylviabishopbooks.com.